MAGIC LILLY

The First Magic Spell

By KNISTER

illustrations by Raimund Frey

Translated by Kathryn Bishop

nedition

This is Lilly. She has a book. It is not an everyday book. It is a book of magic. One day it just mysteriously appeared beside her bed. Just like that.

There are all kinds of magic in this book. There are silly spells and crazy tricks.

But beware…

Don't say the words out loud. Oh no.
For there's no predicting how it could go.

*For if the words aren't exactly right,
the next cookie you try to bite,
might become a sour pickle
or salty fish on pumpernickel.
Your toothbrush might become a broom
with an ugly witch
flying around your room.
Your teacher might*

*become a frog
or a quacking duck
or barking dog.*

Lilly hasn't told anyone about the book. She is a secret magician.

Lilly has a little brother named Leon. He really gets on her nerves sometimes, but she loves him anyway.

Surulunda's Magic Book

Surulunda Knorx is a witch—
an honest-to-goodness magical witch.
But she is a very scatter-
brained witch. And she
has a big problem.

She lost her magic
book—the very one
that Lilly found.
She'll try to get it back,
of course.

One day Lilly was sitting in her room. She was supposed to be doing her homework, but she wasn't in the mood. It was a beautiful, sunny day. Lilly was upset because she wasn't allowed to go outside until her homework was done. And she had a lot of homework—lots of writing and lots of math.

Lilly sat in her room, mumbling to herself and staring up at the ceiling. Suddenly she smiled. She had an idea.

Why should she do math? She had a magic book.

There must be some magic spells that can do homework.

Lilly quickly closed the door. She put her chair under the door handle. She didn't want anyone to come in. She must be alone.

Great Magic Tricks

Lilly was going to try to do magic, so she didn't want to be disturbed. She took out the big heavy book from its secret hiding place. Slowly, she opened it to the first page. There she read a poem.

If you forget what you should do,
this magic book's just right for you.
A bit of dragon, toad, or seashell,
this book will have the perfect spell!

Lilly looked at page after page. She couldn't stop herself. The last ten pages really gave her goose bumps. All of the spells were listed here.

Everything was listed by letter.
Under the letter A was *alligator ambush*.
And under the letter Z was
zig-zagging zombies!

Lilly knew about alligators, but the zig-zagging zombies were completely new. And there were a lot of other things she had never heard of before. And then there were some things that made her hair stand on end.

Lilly knew she wanted to put a spell on her math book. She thought about how to do it.

"Calculate," she thought. "That's a math word, and it starts with C."

So Lilly looked up the letter C. There were several options.

Cats create cacophony (a harsh unpleasant sound).
Calm with catnaps and cream.

Finally, six lines below she found her answer.

Calculate correctly.
Turn to page 1842.

Such a big number for Lilly!

But Lilly was a clever girl. She took each number one at a time. First came the one, then the eight, then the four, and finally the two. A good trick! She easily found the page.

At the top of the page, she found the spell.

Calculate carefully.
You must do it well.
Because it's important,
for each magic spell.

"Of course," thought Lilly. And she read on.

After all, she did want to put a spell on her math book.

Suddenly she heard her mother calling from the kitchen. "Lilly, can you please look after Leon? I have to run to the store."

"I can't," said Lilly. "I have to do my math homework."

But it was too late. Lilly heard the front door close. Her mother had already left.

Always the Little Brother

And sure enough, there was a knock on Lilly's door. It was Leon. Why now? Leon was hopping up and down, making a terrible racket.

"Open up, Lilly," he whined.

"Later. I don't have time now," said Lilly.

Lilly tried to get rid of him, but Leon wouldn't give up.

"Open up! You're suppose to," shouted Leon, pounding on the door. "Mama said so!"

Lilly had no choice. She had to let him in.

"Why did you lock the door?" he asked.

"Because. I don't need you in here," she said.

That didn't stop Leon.

"I want you to play with me," he said.

"I don't have time," said Lilly.

Leon stomped his little feet and shouted, "You have to play with me! Mama said so."

"I don't have to do anything," Lilly snapped, and she kept reading her magic book.

"What are you reading?" asked Leon.

"A book."

"What kind of book?" he asked. "Read me some."

"It's not a book for reading out loud," said Lilly.

She was starting to get mad. But Leon just wouldn't give up. He grabbed the book and started flipping the pages. That was too much. Lilly jumped up and tried to stop him.

Leon ran away. So Lilly chased him. He ran back to the desk. So she chased him around and around.

"You beast!" Lilly yelled at him.

Finally, she was able to grab him by the collar.

"Do you have any idea how hard it was to find the right page?" said Lilly.

Lilly wanted to shake him, but she controlled herself.

"So now what do I do with you?" she said. She was really angry.

"Read to me," said Leon with the friendliest face in the world.

"But I told you this isn't a book for reading out loud," said Lilly.

"Why not? What does it say?" Leon asked.

Then Lilly read something to him just so he would leave her alone.

Lilly Does Magic

Lilly started to read in the middle of the page, right where Leon had opened it.

*To make this work, you'll have to run
three times around the book. It's fun!
A bit of sunshine you'll also need,
but beware of animals. Oh yes, indeed!*

Lilly made up the next line herself.

*Don't be nervous, just be strong.
Tug your ears, and they'll grow long.*

Then Lilly gave her brother's ears a pull.

Oh no! Suddenly Leon started growing two new ears—two long rabbit ears! Lilly couldn't believe her eyes.

"It can't be," she said.

But it was. Instead of his normal ears, Leon had two giant rabbit ears.

"What's the matter?" asked Leon.

He couldn't feel that his ears were different. So Lilly took Leon's hands and put them on his new long ears.

He touched his new ears and said, "Hey, I have long fuzzy ears! Wow! You can do magic!"

Lilly was not as excited as Leon.

"What do I do now?" she said in a small voice.

"Just change them back," said Leon.

Then he said, "Wait. Don't change them back till I show Mama."

Lilly's heart began pounding. She was scared. She didn't know another spell. She didn't know the magic words to turn Leon's ears back to normal. What if it was days before she could find the right spell?

What if Leon's ears stayed that way forever? How would she explain it to her mother?

Lilly tried pulling on Leon's ears. But nothing happened. She had to get rid of those ears before her mother came home.

Lilly tried everything! She pushed and pulled the rabbit ears. She wiggled them back and forth. But nothing happened. They weren't even the slightest bit smaller.

"Oh hoppin' hiccups! Stay calm, Lilly. Don't have a cow," she said to herself.

Vavoosh!

Suddenly Leon had cow's ears. Black and white and pink on the inside.

"Oh no! This can't be happening," said Lilly. "Now, what does Mama always say? Take one step at a time. Don't put the cart before the horse."

Vavoosh!

Leon now had the ears of a horse. But he didn't know what was happening.

Leon touched his ears.

"They're smaller, but still there," he said.

Lilly was so shocked, she couldn't say a thing.

"What's the matter with you?" Leon asked. He was impatient.

"Well, it's just, how should I say it," Lilly said. She was looking for the right words. "Every time I say the name of an animal, your ears change. Right now you have horse's ears."

"Now who's the scaredy cat," giggled Leon.

He tried to touch his horse ears. But with a *vavoosh*, they had changed. Now he had cat ears!

"Wow! I can do magic too," he said.

Leon thought it was great.

Lilly Looks for the Right Words

Lilly tried to think, but it didn't help.
She had to find a spell in the magic
book somewhere. But the book was so
thick. She flipped back and forth through
the pages. Only it just made her more
and more nervous.

It didn't seem to bother Leon at all.
He danced around the room like a cat.
And then he began to do his own magic.

New ears appeared with every
vavoosh.

Kangaroo ears, zebra ears, bat ears, then monkey ears. He had just gotten his elephant ears when Lilly heard the front door open.

"Kids, I'm home!" called Mama.

"Oh, no! We're in trouble now," said Lilly.

"Mama, Mama," called Leon "Look what—"

In a flash, Lilly was right next to her brother. She put her hand over his mouth.

"You say one more word, and I'll take your magic powers away! Do you understand?" whispered Lilly.

Leon nodded. He wanted to keep his new magic powers.

"Did you say something, Leon?"
called Mama.

Lilly quickly put her chair under the
door handle again.

"We're just playing, Mama,"
answered Lilly.

Lilly hoped that would be enough.
And it was, but only for a moment.

And Leon? He was busy wiggling his
new elephant ears.

Lilly flipped through the pages of the magic book as fast as she could. She looked and looked. And suddenly she found what she was looking for.

Need help with a magic problem?
Perhaps this can help!
Abracadabra Quick Help, *the service*
for magic emergencies.
If a spell's turned inside out,
Or magic words are twisted,
Help is on the way.
Any day except Walpurgis Night, and
any time on the sundial…

Abracadabra Quick Help Service for Users of Magic.

Lilly followed the instructions carefully. In a rocking step she danced around the room. She sang the special song she found in the book. And with a *swish* and a *swoosh*, a green column of smoke appeared and then turned into an old lady.

The old lady introduced herself. "Hello, young magician. I'm Surulunda Knorx. How can I help?"

Lilly and Leon didn't know what to say.

Standing in front of them was a real witch! Someone who could do real magic. And this witch was ready for action.

"Creepy crows and stinky feet," she said. "I thought you needed my help. What's the problem?"

"Oh, yes," said Lilly. She felt better already and pointed to Leon.

"Right," said Surulunda. "No problem!"

Surulunda swirled and whirled around Leon. She mumbled some mysterious words. And her magic spell changed Leon—into a little elephant!

"Noooooo! Stop," said Lilly. "That's all wrong. It's worse than before. He is supposed to turn back to normal."

"Who's supposed to be normal?" said Lilly's mother from the kitchen.

"It's okay, Mama," said Lilly quickly.

But it was too late. Mama was now standing in front of Lilly's door, trying to open it.

Luckily, Lilly had put the chair under the door handle.

"Kids, open the door this minute," said Mama

"We're just playing, Mama," said Lilly, hoping that would work.

Just then, Leon began making elephant noises.

"What is going on?" called Mama, knocking loudly on the door.

"Leon?" she said.

Little elephant Leon got louder. He stomped around like any elephant child. The whole apartment started to shake.

There was no stopping Mama now. She was going to come in that room.

Lilly looked at Surulunda. "Please, oh please..."

"I understand," said Surulunda.

Once again, she danced around Lilly's brother. This time it was more difficult. The elephant filled up almost the whole room.

Then with a *swish* and a *swoosh*, Leon was back to normal. He had his own hair, his own skin, and thank goodness, his own ears back.

Lilly Plays Dumb

As fast as she arrived, Surulunda was gone, taking the green column of smoke with her. All with another fast *swish* and *swoosh*!

Surulunda's visit was so short, she didn't even notice her lost magic book. It was still on Lilly's desk.

Suddenly Lilly's chair slipped from under the door handle and Mama was in the room.

"Lilly, Leon, what is going on here?" she asked.

"In here? What do you mean, Mama?" said Lilly.

She was playing dumb, but words spilled out of Leon like a waterfall.

"Mama, you can't imagine, Lilly can do magic!" he said. "First she gave me long rabbit ears and then all kinds of other ears. Then I could do magic too…

"Then there was a real live magic witch, and I was an elephant. And then—"

"Okay, okay," said Mama, laughing. "And I thought something had happened."

She put her arm around Lilly. "It is wonderful how you play so well with your brother," she said.

"Just like always," said Lilly.

"Always?" Mama winked at Lilly. "And I thought he always got on your nerves."

"No, not Leon," said Lilly.